E
WIL   Wilson, Sarah
          Beware the dragons!

    $11.89

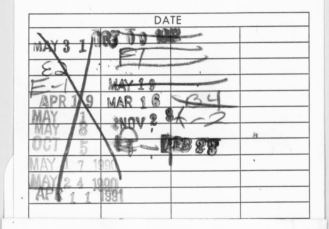

DATE			
MAY 3 1			
APR 1 9	MAY 1 9		
MAY	MAR 1 6	34	
MAY 8	NOV 2	2	
OCT 5	FEB 23		
MAY 1 7 1990			
MAY 2 4 1990			
APR 1 1 1991			

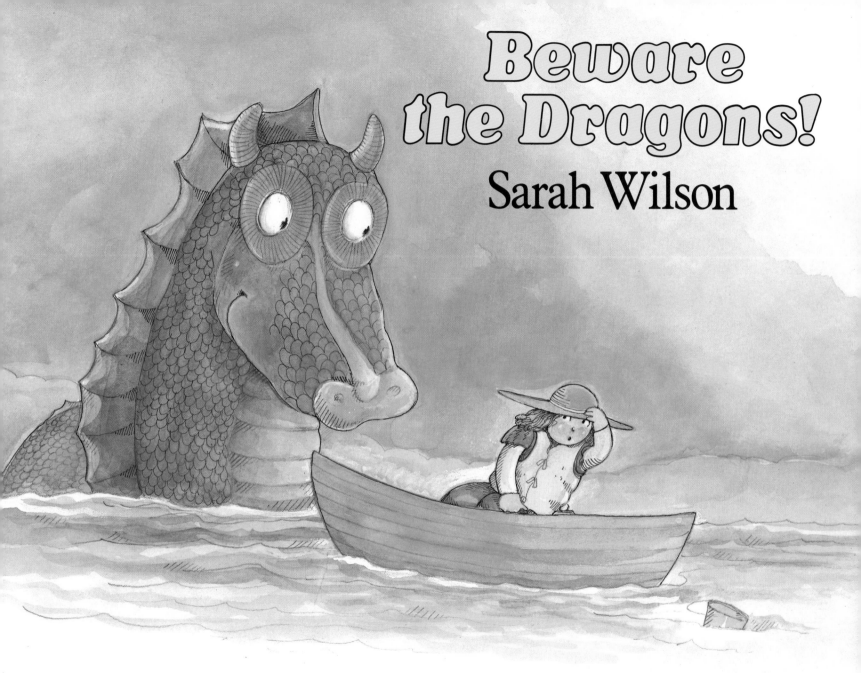

Beware the Dragons!

Sarah Wilson

HARPER & ROW, PUBLISHERS

Library of Congress Cataloging in Publication Data
Wilson, Sarah.
    Beware the dragons!

    Summary: A little girl sets sail across the bay and
discovers that the dragons there, about which her mother
has warned her, only want to play.
    1. Children's stories, American. [1. Dragons—
fiction] I. Title.
PZ7.W6986Be 1985   [E]   85-42614
ISBN 0-06-026508-6
ISBN 0-06-026509-4 (lib. bdg.)

10 9 8 7 6 5 4 3 2 1
First Edition

For my parents

The morning Tildy was to take the boat out alone, there was dragon smoke all over Spooner Bay.

"Great Crying Cuttlefish!" said Tildy. "Why'd they have to come poking around now and spoil my day?"

But by sunup, the smoke had cleared and there wasn't a dragon in sight.

"They're out in the far islands by now," Tildy said. "They won't be back for days! Can I row over to the general store?"

"Will you keep watch for anything green and smoky?" her mother asked.

"Better 'n a keen-eyed gull!" Tildy promised.

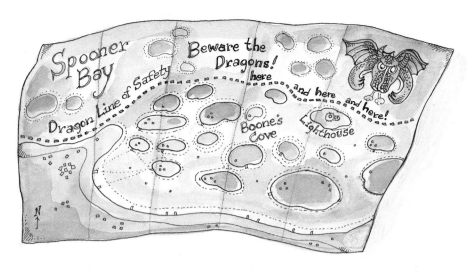

Her mother brought out a map.

"Don't dare drift out near Boone's Cove or toward the lighthouse, Matilda," she said. "Dragons in those parts are as thick as gnats, just set to eat something tasty like a little girl!"

"Haven't heard tell of anybody eaten up yet," Tildy said.

"Doesn't mean there won't be!" warned her mother. "Why else would those fearsome creatures be flying around and around Spooner Bay, scaring folks day and night?"

"Don't know," mumbled Tildy, "but they've hightailed it now, and I've got some sailing to do!"

"Might be some wind coming along too," said her mother. "Maybe even a speck of rain. Row quick, Matilda, and if a storm blows up, stay at the store until it's over."

Tildy was too excited to think about storms. Or dragons, either.

"Right ho!" she shouted, happy to be on her own at last. "I'll be there in the shake of a seal's flipper!"

At first, Tildy rowed quickly.

Then she slowed down to watch some sea gulls.

"Would you like a little lunch, birds?" she asked. "I'm feeling hungry myself!"

With the sun warm on her back, Tildy stopped rowing and forgot all about hurrying, until splat! the first raindrops fell on her nose.

Soon, most of the sky had turned ink dark and a mean wind was gusting up around her.

"Whooeee!" Tildy yelled at the storm. "Where'd *you* come from?"

Things quickly went from bad to worse. The wind and waves carried her little boat on and on, far out into the bay, until suddenly—far from land and smack in the middle of nowhere—the boat hit a bump.

Tildy couldn't see a thing in all the rain and mist.

"Shivering Shark Tails!" she grumbled, keeping still until the storm finally cleared. But when the bump leaned to one side, Tildy sat up, and looked around, and let out one wild whooping yell.

"YEOWWW! DRAGONS!" she hollered. "Great Mustard Greens and Shooting Stars, I'm stuck on a dragon-bump!"

Before Tildy could blink her eyes, the dragons had tossed her out of the boat and up in the air like a sky rocket!

The boat came flying up after her.

"HELPPP!" Tildy yelled, but, except for the dragons, there was no one around to hear her.

Then she heard what sounded like laughing. Dragons laughing. Big hearty roars, followed by lots of bubbling and gurgling.

The laughter grew louder. It was plain to see that the dragons were having a very good time.

Tildy wasn't. Not one bit.

"Leaping Lobsters!" Tildy gasped, shooting up in the air again. And again after that.

When she finally caught her breath, Tildy wasn't scared anymore. She was mad! Red-faced, squinty-eyed mad.

"STOP THAT! You horrible mean nasty bullies!" she shouted down at them. "You wouldn't be so brave if there were folks around to help me! PUT ME DOWN!"

So they did. And with a big splash.

"We're very sorry," said a dragon who introduced himself as Jebediah. "We thought you came out to play with us!"

"PLAY with you?" Tildy sputtered. "Great Snapping Sea Turtles, you're as big as houses!"

"I suppose that's why *nobody* ever comes out to play with us. Nobody likes us!" Jebediah looked like he wanted to cry.

To Tildy's amazement, some of the other dragons did cry.

"It's as lonesome as winter out here with no one to visit!" sobbed a dragon with white whiskers. "Nothing but the wind yowling and no games to play and no new stories to hear, ever."

"So *that's* why you come to Spooner Bay!" Tildy exclaimed. "We thought you wanted to eat us!"

"Dragons don't eat people," said Jebediah. "We eat seaweed and crushed rock and old campfires!" And he started to cry, too.

Tildy felt terrible.

"Suffering Squid!" she said.

"Folks in the Bay don't dislike dragons, they're just afraid. If you'll help me get home, I have an idea how to set things right and proper."

The dragons decided that one idea was better than no ideas at all.

"Please ask the dragons to go orderly, now," Tildy told the old dragon with whiskers. "Too much smoke and fire and roaring around is what gets to scaring folks!"

Bravely, they escorted Tildy back into Spooner Bay. It turned out to be the biggest excitement for as long as anyone could remember.

"Better 'n the Fourth of July!" Tildy shouted to Jebediah, riding up on top like a queen of the sea, waving at the people on shore.

When they reached land, Tildy ran quickly to Mr. Scott's General Store.

"They're really very nice dragons," she said, all in one breath, "not mean and ornery, just lonesome! What they need now is big rubber balls and water kites and rafts. And anything else that floats, please."

Two people fainted.

"Balls and kites and rafts?" stammered Mr. Scott. But he and the other townspeople were too scared to say no, not with a whole bay full of dragons outside. They gave Tildy everything she asked for.

Then, while everybody on shore waited breathlessly to see what would happen next, the dragons began to play—really play—for the first time in all their hundreds of years! They flew kites on their horns. They played slide-the-ball-down-your-scales. They had raft races.

"Well, I'll be a cross-eyed barnacle!" muttered Mr. Scott. "Those dragons look about as fearsome as a pack of pond otters! A mite large, maybe, but what's the harm?"

The other townspeople were shocked and puzzled and then relieved. They began to smile.

Children begged to go out and play with Tildy.

There was a town meeting, later, before sundown.

"Please let the dragons stay," Tildy begged. "They mean no harm. They're just plain lonesome."

Mr. Scott spoke for the townspeople. "About time we had some peace around here!" he said. "For our part, we'll see that no dragon lacks for good company or games."

Everybody cheered.

For the first time in more years than anyone wanted to count, there was nothing to be feared in Spooner Bay.

"Starbursters!" Tildy sighed gratefully. "The day turned out right, after all!"

But the best part came the next morning, when there was dragon smoke over Spooner Bay and no one seemed to mind.

Least of all Tildy.

She was, of course, a hero.